Roger Smit

Gordon Goes to School

Oxford University Press
Oxford Toronto Melbourne

Oxford University Press, Walton Street, Oxford OX2 6DP
Oxford London Glasgow
New York Toronto Melbourne Auckland
Kuala Lumpur Singapore Hong Kong Tokyo
Delhi Bombay Calcutta Madras Karachi
Nairobi Dar es Salaam Cape Town
and associated companies in
Beirut Berlin Ibadan Mexico City Nicosia

Oxford is a trade mark of Oxford University Press

© Roger Smith 1984
An Umbrella Book Series Editor: Jill Bennett
First published 1984

All rights reserved. No part of this publication may be reproduced, stored in a retrieval system, or transmitted, in any form, or by any means electronic, mechanical, photocopying, recording, or otherwise, without the prior permission of Oxford University Press

This book is sold subject to the condition that it shall not, by way of trade or otherwise, be lent, re-sold, hired or otherwise circulated, without the publisher's prior consent in any form of binding or cover other than that in which it is published and without a similar condition including this condition being imposed on the subsequent purchaser

British Library Cataloguing in Publication Data
Smith, Roger, 1930 Mar. 15–
Gordon goes to school.
I. Title
823'.914[j] P27
ISBN 0-19-278202-9

Typeset by Oxford Publishing Services, Oxford
Printed in Hong Kong

It was Gordon's first day at school.
'You must never EVER forget,' said Gordon's mother. 'Elephants *never* forget.'

'Forget what?' asked Gordon.
'You mustn't forget anything,'
said Gordon's mother.

'Don't forget – your buns for playtime, or my birthday, or to clean your teeth and tusks every day, or to give up your seat to old ladies on the bus.'

'But I've got a memory like a-a-'
said Gordon.
'A sieve!' said his mother.

They set off for the school.
'Dinner money,' said Gordon's mother.
'What about dinner money?' said Gordon.

They walked along the pavement.
'Have you got it?' said Gordon's mother.
Gordon thought for a bit.

'You gave it to me with my clean handkerchief.'
'That's better,' said Gordon's mother.
'You can remember things.
Where is your hanky now?'

Gordon searched his pockets.
'I've lost it,' he said at last.
'I definitely remember losing it.'
'When?' said Gordon's mother.

They stopped at the zebra crossing.
'When what?' said Gordon.
'When did you lose it?'
'Lose what?' said Gordon.

'Your handkerchief,' said Gordon's mother. 'Or was it your dinner money? Or both? *I've* forgotten what we were talking about now!'

'You really must try to remember, Mum,' said Gordon.
'You've got a memory like a sieve.'

When Gordon got to school he met his teacher.
Her name was Miss Snibbs.

'So you're Gordon,' she said.
'Yes,' said Gordon.

'Yes what?' said Miss Snibbs.
'Yes, my name's Gordon,' said Gordon patiently.

'It's always just been Gordon.'

'Yes, *Miss Snibbs*,' said Miss Snibbs,
'You can call me *Miss Snibbs*,
or if you prefer it, *Miss*.
You must try not to forget it.' She paused.

'Now what's my name, dear?'
asked Miss Snibbs.
She's as bad as me, thought Gordon,
and she's the teacher!

'Miss Snibbs, Miss,' shouted all the class.

'You'll remember it in the end,'
said Gordon kindly.

When they were in class Miss Snibbs put on her glasses.
'Today, children, we will learn to spell,' she said.

'We'll start with a very easy word.'

She turned and wrote **cat** in large chalk letters on the blackboard.
'**c** for cream,
a for apples,
t for toffee,' she said.

Gordon was thinking about toffee apples
covered in cream.
Miss Snibbs rubbed the letters off
the blackboard.
'How do you spell cat then, Gordon?'
she asked.

'You've just told us, Miss,' said Gordon.
'You can't have forgotten already.
But don't worry. There's a word for people with our sort of trouble.'

'It's spelt – **a** for aniseed balls,
m for milk shakes, **n** for nutty bars,
e for eclairs, **s** for sticky buns, **i** for iced lollies,
a for acid drops. It's called **amnesia**
and it means loss of memory.'

'I'll speak to you later – whatever-your-name-is!' squeaked Miss Snibbs.

Gordon's mother met him from school.
'How did you get on, dear?' she asked.
'Did you learn a lot?'

'Well I think I was quite a help to
our teacher,' said Gordon.
'Poor thing, her memory is
even worse than mine.'

'But she did say that after only one day in her class, she would remember *me* for the rest of her life!'